James Mayhew

presents

Ella Bella

BALLERINA

~ and ~

Swan Lake

zoey

For Lesley Agnew
~ Bookseller extraordinaire ~
and
for Rosalind Sippy
~ Also a wonderful bookseller ~
(and ballet costumier)

With thanks and love
J. M.

ORCHARD BOOKS
338 Euston Road, London, NW1 3BH
Orchard Books Australia
Level 17/207 Kent Street, Sydney, NSW 2000

First published in 2010 by Orchard Books
First published in paperback in 2011
Text and illustrations © James Mayhew 2010

ISBN 978 1 40830 077 0

A CIP catalogue record for this book
is available from the British Library.

4 6 8 10 9 7 5 3

Printed in China

Orchard Books is a division of Hachette Children's Books,
an Hachette UK company.
www.hachette.co.uk

James Mayhew
presents

Ella Bella
❋ BALLERINA ❋
~ and ~
Swan Lake

ORCHARD

It was pouring with rain when Ella Bella arrived
at the old theatre for her ballet lesson.
"Come in, darling," said Madame Rosa, her
teacher. "It's lovely and warm inside."

Ella Bella changed into her
ballet shoes and joined
the rest of the class.

"Now, my darlings," said Madame Rosa, fetching her musical box, "today we shall dance to the music from *Swan Lake*."
"That's a pretty name for a ballet," smiled Ella Bella. "Does it have any princesses?"

"Of course!" said Madame Rosa. "There is a swan princess!"

Inside the beautiful box, the little ballerina spun
around and magnificent music began to play.
The children all imagined they were baby swans
and danced around the stage.

"Will you tell us about the swan princess?"
asked the children.
"Well, her name was Odette," said Madame Rosa.
"A wicked sorcerer turned her into a swan and only
at night was she allowed to be a princess again."

"Couldn't the spell be broken?" asked Ella Bella.
"Only with the promise of true love," replied
Madame Rosa. "And one night, Odette met a
handsome prince, but the wicked sorcerer tried
to stop them falling in love . . ."

Just then, the music finished.
"Goodness! Time to get
changed, children," called
Madame Rosa. "Off we go."
But Ella Bella stayed behind
on the big empty stage,
all by herself.

Gently, she lifted the lid
of Madame Rosa's box.
The little ballerina inside
twirled. Then, the *Swan Lake*
music began to play and,
as Ella Bella danced around,
it grew louder and louder!

Suddenly, Ella Bella saw something flying down towards her! It was a flock of white swans, shimmering in the moonlight!

As they landed beside a lake, the swans turned into
beautiful ballerinas. One of them wore a crown.
"You must be the Swan Princess!"
said Ella Bella, curtseying.

"Yes, I'm Princess Odette," the Swan Princess whispered shyly. "And my beloved prince is waiting at the castle. He promised to declare his love for me at the Royal Ball tonight!"
"Would that break the sorcerer's spell?" asked Ella Bella.

"It would," said Odette, "but if
the sorcerer finds out, he will try to
stop the prince from declaring his love."
"Let's make sure the sorcerer isn't there,"
said Ella Bella. "I'll go with you."
They set off for the castle together.

Ella Bella left Odette outside and stepped into the dazzling ballroom. She could see no one who looked like a sorcerer. Instead, what a sight met her eyes!

Princesses from all over the world danced for the prince. But he seemed to be waiting for someone special . . .

Just then, a tall baron in a long feathery cape
arrived with another princess. She looked exactly
like Odette, but she was dressed in black, and
her eyes flashed as she looked at the prince.
"Please, may I have this dance?" he asked her.
"That *can't* be Odette," thought Ella Bella.
"She was wearing white!"

Ella Bella curtseyed to the prince.
"Excuse me, Your Highness . . ." she began.
But the prince didn't seem to hear her.
"I give this princess my promise of true love!"
he declared.

"But look!" said Ella Bella, pointing.
The prince suddenly saw the real Odette,
fluttering helplessly at the window!

The baron began to laugh. He revealed that
he was the sorcerer and he had cast a magic spell
to make his daughter, Odile, look like Odette!

Ella Bella and the prince rushed outside,
but Odette had gone! They quickly ran
down to the lake to search for her.

They found Odette hiding in the reeds
with the other swan-maidens.

"You've promised your love to another," she wept.
"At sunrise I will become a swan forever!"
"But I was tricked by the sorcerer," said the
prince. "It's you I love. We must never be
parted again!"

But just then, the angry sorcerer appeared!
He summoned a terrible storm to keep
the prince and Odette apart.

Odette leapt into the lake to escape the sorcerer's clutches.

The prince fought with the sorcerer and threw him to the ground before bravely leaping after Odette!

The storm cleared and, as the sun rose, Ella Bella saw Odette in the arms of the prince. Even though it was morning, she had not turned into a swan!

"True love has destroyed the sorcerer's magic!"
smiled Odette. "Thank you, Ella Bella, and farewell!"
Music filled the air as Ella Bella watched Odette and
the prince sail across the lake, happy and in love.

Ella Bella twirled around . . . but realised the music
had stopped. She was all alone on the empty stage.
Ella slowly closed the lid of the musical box.

"Are you still here?" said Madame Rosa, peeping around the doorway. "Your mamma is waiting for you."

Ella Bella told Madame Rosa about Odette and her prince.
"It's a beautiful story," said Madame Rosa.
"I'm sure they lived happily ever after."
"Of course they did!" laughed Ella Bella.

"Now, good night my little swan-girl,"
said Madame Rosa. "Don't forget to practise
your dancing."

"I won't," said Ella Bella. "Good night!"
And she danced and splashed in the puddles
all the way home, just like a baby swan.

Swan Lake is the most famous classical ballet in the world.

Its beautiful and haunting music is by the great Russian composer Peter Tchaikovsky. The idea grew out of a children's ballet called *The Lake of Swans*, which he wrote for his niece and nephew to perform at home. Then, in 1875-6 Tchaikovsky turned it into a proper ballet in four acts for the magnificent Bolshoi Theatre in Moscow, Russia.

Swan Lake was Tchaikovsky's very first ballet. At first, some people thought it was too hard to dance to the music and it was only after Tchaikovsky's death that *Swan Lake* became truly successful. In 1895, the ballet steps (choreography) and the story were changed, and a new performance took place in St Petersburg, Russia. This time the ballet was a triumph.

Over the years, new ideas have been added and now lots of different versions of the story exist. Sometimes there is a tragic ending where the prince (who is called Siegfried) and Odette are reunited in heaven. Often the wicked baron (who is called Von Rothbart) can use magic to turn himself into an owl, and Odile, his daughter, into a black swan.

Odette and Odile are performed by the same dancer. Nowadays, every great ballerina longs to play the double role of the white and black swans. Although it's a very challenging part that requires great strength, a really good ballerina can be as graceful and elegant as a real swan.